SEVEN WEIRD DAYS AT

Judy Allen has written more than fifty books – fiction and non-fiction – for adults and children. Her stories for children include *Auntie Billie's Greatest Invention*, *The Most Brilliant Trick Ever*, *The Dim Thin Ducks*, *The Great Pig Sprint*, *The Dream Thing*, *Something Rare and Special*, *Travelling Hopefully* and *Awaiting Developments*, which won the Whitbread Award and the Friends of the Earth Earthworm Award. She has a particular interest in ecological issues and is the author of six Animals at Risk books – *Tiger*, *Panda*, *Whale*, *Elephant*, *Eagle* and *Seal* – and the compiler of *Anthology for the Earth*. She has also written two adult novels, one of which, *December Flower*, was made into a television film.

Books by the same author

SEVEN WEIRD DAYS AT NUMBER 31

JUDY ALLEN

Illustrations by
DEREK BRAZELL

WALKER BOOKS
AND SUBSIDIARIES
LONDON • BOSTON • SYDNEY

First published 1998 by Walker Books Ltd
87 Vauxhall Walk, London SE11 5HJ

This edition published 1998

2 4 6 8 10 9 7 5 3 1

This book has been typeset in Plantin.

Printed in England

British Library Cataloguing in Publication Data
A catalogue record for this book is available
from the British Library.

ISBN 0-7445-6025-X

Contents

Chapter 1

Day and Night One

....

Mike watched in amazement as everything he owned flew out of his bedroom window and landed at his feet.

He and Scott had just carried it all up there. Now here it was, in a heap in the front garden.

His mother appeared at the open front door. "Don't leave your clothes on the grass!" she said.

Scott's mother appeared beside her and they both hurried past him to the removal van which the two fathers were busy unloading.

Mike sighed and scooped up as many of his clothes as he could carry in one go. He thought he knew what had happened.

He hadn't wanted to move to Number 31 South Street. Scott hadn't wanted him to move either. They had both liked being in the same block of flats, almost next-door neighbours. Mike was sure Scott had decided to stage a protest.

He staggered in at the front door, trying not to tread on a trailing jacket sleeve.

A ginger cat pushed past him on its way out. Mike wasn't surprised. There were flaps in the front and back doors, and he'd already discovered that the local cats used the house as a walk-through.

"Come on, Scott," he said as he went into his room. "Help me get the rest of it."

Then he stood still, feeling stupid. There was no one in there.

He dumped the things on his bed and went downstairs again, feeling puzzled.

In the front garden he found Scott staring at the heap on the ground.

"It WAS you, wasn't it?" said Mike. "You did chuck all this out of the window?"

Scott looked at him in amazement. "Of course I didn't!" he said. "Why would I?"

They hurried upstairs and began to conduct some experiments to see how the stuff could have fallen out of the window by itself. Their best theory was that it had been stacked in such a crooked pile on the bed under the window that it had simply overbalanced. Annoyingly, none of the experiments worked. No matter how crookedly they stacked Mike's possessions, and no matter how much they jumped up and down and slammed the bedroom door to create vibrations, all his things remained stubbornly inside his room.

After a while they gave up.

"Probably a cat pushed it," said Mike, remembering the feline through-way.

"Or a freak whirlwind," said Scott, who preferred a more dramatic explanation.

When the van was empty and everything was in the house, Mike's father bought fish and chips for all six of them. They ate it in the front room which was full of the last owner's furniture.

Mike's mother had explained this to him. "We didn't have enough in the old flat to furnish all these rooms," she'd said. "So we bought this with the house."

There were several old chairs, a huge sofa, a wooden table with feet like lion's claws, a glass-fronted cupboard, a padded footstool and a clock with Roman numerals around its face.

When the clock began to strike it made such a noise that Mike choked on a piece of batter and Scott knocked over the vinegar bottle.

"That's LOUD," said Scott's mother.

By the time it had reached seven, Mike's father had worked out how to open the back and switch off the chimes.

"It's a nice clock," said Scott's father. "When it isn't striking."

"It'll never strike again," said Mike's father. "I've fixed it."

Not long after that, Scott and his parents went home and Mike's parents looked at the silent clock and said it was late and time to say goodnight.

It wasn't until Mike was actually in bed, and had turned out his reading lamp, that he discovered he didn't like being in a strange room in the dark. He had never been nervous of the dark before, and he was surprised. He reached out and switched the lamp on again.

A bit later, his father put his head round the bedroom door. "Lights out," he said. "School tomorrow."

"Can I leave the landing light on?" said Mike. He didn't want to admit he was scared, so he added hastily, "In case I can't find the bathroom in the night."

"Fine," said his father.

The line of light under the bedroom door was reassuring, and Mike relaxed.

It was the clock down in the sitting-room that woke him, chiming four. When he opened his eyes, he was shocked at how dark it was. One of his parents must have turned off the landing light by mistake.

He was aware of the other sounds even before he found the switch on the bedside lamp. They were very quiet, but he knew what they were at once. They were footsteps.

Soft, quick footsteps were coming up the stairs. They padded along the landing to his door – and then stopped outside.

When the moaning started it was so low Mike could hardly hear it above the thudding of his own heart. He gripped the edge of the duvet and waited for whatever it was to come into his room. Nothing happened.

The next second, he heard his parents' bedroom door open. A switch clicked and the comforting line of light reappeared under his own door. The moaning stopped abruptly.

Mike scrambled out of bed and went on to the landing. There was nothing strange to be seen anywhere. Just his father, heading for the stairs, looking cross and sleepy. "That was a silly trick," he muttered.

"What was?" said Mike. He didn't want to be left alone on the landing so he followed his father down to the sitting-room.

"Switching the chiming mechanism on again," said his father. He swivelled the clock around, opened the back, and adjusted something inside.

"I didn't!" said Mike.

"We heard you moving about," said his father. He yawned and began to plod back upstairs.

"It wasn't me!" said Mike, following him. "I heard footsteps too. I think it was some kind of animal. It came right up to my door."

"Cats," said his father. "If they're going to be a nuisance we'll have to stop them coming through."

"It wasn't a cat," said Mike. "You can't hear a cat walk. Anyway, it wasn't a cat that messed with the clock."

"Exactly!" said his father, giving him a straight look.

"You should believe me!" said Mike. "It isn't fair!"

"We'll talk about it in the morning," said

his father. "Go back to bed."

Mike was convinced he was too churned up ever to sleep again. But he knew he had to stay in his room and pretend, so he got into bed and lay down. This time he took no chances. He left the bedside lamp on.

The next thing he knew, his mother was calling that it was time to get up.

Neither of his parents said anything about the night before. They had obviously decided to pretend nothing had happened. Mike decided to do the same. In fact he even began to convince himself he'd imagined the padding feet and the faint moaning, crying sounds.

He swallowed some breakfast and went back up to his room to fetch his schoolbag.

That was when he saw them. Deep, long scratch marks, all over the outside of his bedroom door.

Chapter 2

Day Two

....

Mike's father was certain the scratches had already been on the outside of Mike's door when they moved in. "Don't worry," he said. "We'll redecorate."

"You don't understand," said Mike, who was equally certain the scratches hadn't been there when they moved in. "I *heard* something outside my door. It came up the stairs just after the clock woke me."

"You're pushing your luck," said his father. "We'd decided to forget about the clock episode – as long as you don't do it again."

Mike opened his mouth to say he hadn't done it the first time. Then he shut it again. They were determined to think it was him. And there was no way he could prove it wasn't. Also, all three of them were caught up in the usual rush to get to work and school and he knew it wasn't the moment to get anyone's attention.

"This evening," said his mother, "when we've got more time, I want us to search the house for cats. Then I'm shutting those cat doors for good."

"I think this house is haunted," said Mike, but at that moment the postman loomed up on the other side of the glass front door and several envelopes slithered through on to the mat.

There were three "Welcome To Your New Home" cards, a leaflet for a Pizza Home Delivery service and an airmail letter for someone called N. Dark.

"Who's this?" said Mike's father, turning it over in his hands. "I thought the last owner's name was Mrs Mullish."

"It was," said Mike's mother.

"There's an address on the back," said Mike's father. "I'll write 'Return To Sender' on it and post it."

"Maybe it's for one of the neighbours,"

said his mother. "Leave it for now – we can ask around later. Come on, let's go, we're all going to be late."

Mike hardly bothered to listen. He had something else on his mind.

There was another reason he hadn't wanted to move, apart from the fact that he wouldn't live near Scott any more. He'd been trying not to think about this other thing, but he knew he'd have to face up to it any minute now.

He walked down the path, out of the gate and along the pavement to the corner. Here he paused and looked both ways. He didn't see what he was looking for, so he went on, along beside the main road, his head full of the noise of traffic.

He wondered if, by chance, he'd timed things right. Perhaps there wasn't going to be a problem after all. Or, at least, not today. Then, as he passed the paper shop, a figure bounced out of the doorway, peeling the wrapper off a chocolate bar.

"You walk my way to school now," it announced.

Mike sighed. This was it. The other reason he hadn't wanted to move.

Greg.

Greg who most people tried to avoid. Greg who couldn't easily be avoided now that Mike's route to school ran right past his home.

"If you want some of this chocolate you'll have to fight me for it," said Greg, falling into step beside him.

"I don't want any," said Mike.

"Are you scared of me?" said Greg, edging Mike over until he was jammed against a lamppost.

"No," said Mike, wriggling free and walking on.

"You're shorter than me," said Greg.

"I know," said Mike.

"You're shorter than everyone in our class," said Greg.

"I know," said Mike.

"Is there something wrong with you?" said Greg.

"No," said Mike.

It wasn't a very long walk to school, but he could tell it was going to seem like miles and miles. And he had to do it every single day.

"Well why are you shorter, then?" Greg persisted.

"People come in different sizes," said Mike wearily.

Greg wasn't exactly a bully, although he did push people around sometimes. The main problem was that he was incredibly annoying. He'd been at the school for two terms now, but it had only taken a week for everyone to decide they didn't like him.

The teachers didn't seem to like him much, either. It wasn't that he made trouble, or was lazy, or lied about having lost his homework, or any of the usual things. It was that he annoyed them as well.

He told Mr Austin that he had hair growing out of his ears. This was perfectly true, but not something Mr Austin liked having pointed out.

He told Miss Wishart that her car was a rusty wreck, Mrs Prendergast that he knew her skirt must be old because the seat was all shiny, and Mr Shipsey that it wasn't possible to say his name without spitting.

Traditionally, anyone who got on the wrong side of the teachers automatically got on the right side of his classmates. In Greg's case, though, that didn't work. Everyone simply avoided him, which was easy enough – usually.

By the time they were walking in at the school gates, Mike was promising himself he would work out a different route, even if it meant climbing over the rooftops.

He'd arrived so late that he didn't get a chance to tell Scott about the sounds and scratch marks until they were eating their sandwiches at lunchtime.

He would have been very unhappy if Scott had disbelieved him. Even so, he found he wasn't exactly happy when Scott said, "You're right. It's haunted. That house is definitely haunted."

Chapter 3

Night Two

Mike remembered Scott's words several times that evening, but he didn't say anything to his parents. They were too busy unpacking. He took his homework to his room and kept out of their way.

As far as he was concerned, the only nice thing that happened was that they had fish and chips for the second day running.

Before he went to bed he stuck a piece of sticky tape over the landing light switch. That way none of them could turn it off accidentally.

The clock in the sitting-room didn't wait until four in the morning this time. It chimed at three.

Mike sat up in his dark bedroom, staring at the line of light under his door and waiting for the padding steps and the crying sound.

They didn't happen. Nor did either of his parents come out of their room.

According to his watch, he sat listening and wondering for over half an hour before he made the decision to go downstairs.

He guessed his parents had slept through the noise, but they might not sleep through the next chiming, or the one after that. It seemed like a really good idea to switch off the clock. Also, he thought he might be able to discover some technical fault that would prove that the clock had somehow reactivated its own striking mechanism.

He opened his bedroom door as quietly as he could and looked around the landing and down the stairs. Everything seemed perfectly normal.

He went down to the sitting-room slowly, testing each stair in case it creaked. He didn't want to wake his parents before he'd sorted things out.

The mantelpiece was high and the clock was large. He had to stand on the padded footstool to look into the back of it. He could see at once what had to be done. There was a small lever which moved the striking hammer. With the lever pushed one way, the hammer would strike the bell when the clockwork told it to. With the lever pushed the other way the hammer would miss the bell and swipe silently at empty space.

Mike switched the lever into the "off" position. It was quite stiff. He couldn't see how it could possibly have slipped back to the "on" position by itself. Twice.

While he was still thinking about this, he heard something. It wasn't anything much, just a brief chinking sound, as if someone had knocked a mug against a plate. It came from behind the door that led into the kitchen.

He closed the back of the clock and swivelled it into position as quietly as he could, listening all the time. As he stepped down from the footstool he was sure he heard something else, something soft and muffled.

"Cats," he thought. "I hope."

He stood still for a moment, wondering which was worse. To go back to bed not knowing what might be in the kitchen. Or to open the door and look inside. His parents suddenly seemed a long way away, upstairs in their room. Also, he suddenly remembered they'd locked both cat flaps. Not cats, then.

He went over to the kitchen door and listened. Nothing. He put his ear right against the wooden panels but still he couldn't hear a thing.

He took a deep breath and opened the door. There was a nasty moment when he had to reach into the dark room to turn on the light. He managed, though, and stood there in the doorway looking about him.

Nothing moved in the kitchen. Everything looked normal.

Or almost normal.

He took a few steps into the room. There was an empty dog dish in the middle of the table. His family had never had a dog, therefore they had never had a dog dish. It wasn't theirs.

Also he distinctly remembered his mother telling him the mugs belonged on the bottom shelf of the wall cupboard, and would he please put his away when he'd finished with it. But now the mugs were standing in a row on the windowsill.

Then something happened which he could never explain properly, even to Scott. He suddenly knew that the kitchen was angry with him. No, not the kitchen, someone in the kitchen. Yet there was no one in the kitchen.

The feeling was very strong. It paralysed him. He wanted to run back upstairs but he couldn't. He couldn't do anything.

The spell was broken unexpectedly by a mewing and scrabbling on the other side of the back door. A cat was trying to get through the locked flap.

It sounded so desperate that Mike automatically moved to let it in. Instantly, the angry feeling went away. Surprised, but very relieved, Mike unbolted the cat door and stood aside as a large tabby pushed its way through. It didn't seem to sense anything strange in the kitchen. He followed it to the front door and let it out that way.

He considered bolting both cat doors again. Then he abandoned the idea. After all, it wasn't a cat that had moaned at his door the night before, it wasn't a cat that had made the clock chime, it wasn't a cat that was angry with him in the kitchen. Why make the cats' lives difficult when none of the weird events were their fault?

Mike hurried back up to his room. Once inside he closed the door and stood a chair against it, just in case. Then he got into bed and pulled the duvet over his head.

In the warm darkness he drifted off into a deep and peaceful sleep.

He didn't wake when it got stuffy under the duvet. He just pushed it down a bit in his sleep.

In fact he slept so deeply and peacefully that, this time, he didn't hear the footsteps padding up the stairs and across the landing.

He was completely unaware that something slipped through his closed door, and through the chair, as easily as if they hadn't been there.

He never knew that it prowled silently around the room and stopped beside his bed.

He didn't even wake when it sniffed at his hand two or three times – and then vanished, as suddenly as if someone had switched it off.

Chapter 4

Day Three

Day three in the new house started really badly.

Mike was in trouble for moving all kinds of things in the kitchen. He was in trouble for bringing in the old, dirty dog dish from the back garden. Finally, he was in trouble for unbolting the cat doors.

"You can forget about having Scott over after school tonight," said his father.

"But he's already invited!" said Mike.

"Then you'll have to uninvite him," said his mother. "You can't expect to get away with behaviour like that without being punished."

"I didn't do ANY of it," said Mike. "Except let a cat through. I want Scott to come over. It isn't fair."

When he thought about it later, he realized he must have looked as upset as he felt.

"Well," said his father reluctantly, "I'll think about it."

"Perhaps," said his mother cautiously, "if you *promise* not to do any of these stupid things again…"

Mike decided to take that to mean Scott was reinvited. He left hurriedly before either of them could say any more.

He had entirely forgotten he had meant to find another route to school. So he took the obvious one and had an irritating walk with Greg, who kept pushing him.

"Don't DO that," said Mike.

"Why don't you push me back?" said Greg.

Infuriated, Mike did just that. He lunged at Greg with his shoulder, meaning to shove him really hard. But at the last second Greg sidestepped and Mike lurched straight past him and into a house wall.

He thought Greg would never stop laughing.

"It wasn't that funny," said Mike. "Nothing's *that* funny."

However, he and Scott had worked out how to avoid walking home with Greg that evening. They had arranged to stay on late, with the people who chose to do their homework at school.

Even that almost didn't work. Greg walked over and leaned on Mike's desk.

"I'll stay too, shall I?" he said.

"No," said Mike and Scott together.

"But if I stay, me and Mike can walk home together," said Greg.

"No," said Mike, again.

"Shove off," said Scott.

"You won't get good marks just because you're doing your homework in school," said Greg spitefully. "It's maths. You always get bad marks in maths. Both of you."

They ignored him.

He hung around for several minutes more, but at last he left.

Later, back at Mike's house, the atmosphere was almost cheerful. Mike's parents were in a good mood again. Scott was happy to get another look at the house now that he'd heard about the second stage of odd happenings. Only Mike was subdued.

He understood that, once again, his parents had decided to pretend that nothing awkward had happened. Since that was their way of dealing with things, he thought, there really was no point trying to persuade them the house was haunted. They simply wouldn't want to know.

"By the way," Mike's mother remarked to his father across the Home-Delivered Pizza, "I asked the neighbours about that letter. The one for N. Dark, remember? Apparently Mrs Mullish had lodgers and N. Dark was one of them. They don't have a forwarding address though."

"Oh well," said Mike's father. "We'd better 'Return to Sender' after all."

After the pizza, Mike and Scott went out to the garden, where they could talk in private.

"You didn't tell me about the letter," said Scott urgently. "That could be important."

"I forgot," said Mike.

"There might be more to this than just a haunted house," said Scott.

"How do you mean?"

"N. Dark!" said Scott. "Think about it. Is that a weird name or is that a weird name?"

"I suppose it is," said Mike.

"The lodger might have been involved in – you know – PRACTICES!" said Scott.

"What practices?"

"I don't know," said Scott. "Witchcraft. Calling things up."

"You mean, like, demons?"

"Could be. And it could be that N. Dark had your room. That seems to be the centre of things."

"Do you mind! I have to live here. I have to sleep here, at night, in the dark, with clocks chiming and something padding around. I'd rather think it was cats."

"You said yourself – you don't hear cats walk."

"That tabby one last night was very big,"

said Mike hopefully. "And it was definitely a cat. A normal, ordinary, furry, stripy cat."

Scott shook his head. "That wasn't a cat you heard walking up the stairs," he said. "I think that was a dog. A large dog. The dog that used to eat out of that dish – when it was still alive."

"Oh, please!" said Mike.

"And I've just realized – this house is Number Thirty-One, right? Well thirty-one is thirteen backwards. Thirteen is a *really* dodgy number. Don't you think?"

"I think I wish you hadn't come back this evening," said Mike.

At that moment his mother leaned out of the kitchen window. "Scott," she called. "Your father's here to collect you."

"OK," Scott called back.

Then, as he and Mike went indoors, he said quietly, "Let's go up to your room one more time. See if the lodger left any clues. Anything we didn't notice before."

"We'll have to be quick, then," said Mike.

"I'm in enough trouble. I don't want to be told off for keeping your dad waiting."

Neither of them knew what they were looking for at the top of the stairs. And neither of them expected what they found.

Everything Mike owned had been flung out of his bedroom and lay in messy piles on the landing outside his door.

Chapter 5

Night Three and Day Four

....

There was only just time to get Mike's stuff back in his room, any old how, before Scott had to leave with his father.

But at least that way no adult saw the mess and Mike didn't get the blame.

He spent an hour putting everything back where he wanted it and closing every drawer and cupboard door again. Then he sat quietly, waiting until he heard his parents go to bed.

He had worked out that, as far as he knew, nothing odd had so far happened in the bathroom, his parents' room, or the spare room. The first two were no good. As soon as all was quiet he crept along the corridor to the spare room, with his pillow under his arm, his alarm clock in his pocket, and his duvet trailing behind him.

The bed wasn't made up, but he rolled himself in his duvet and slept well. The sitting-room clock remained silent. The night was beautifully uneventful.

Mike got up as soon as his alarm clock woke him, early enough to move himself and his bedding back to his own room before his parents were around.

He had a second good reason for getting up early. He had decided to walk to school at least half an hour before his usual time.

"Why?" said his father.

"Because if I go at the usual time I have to walk with Greg," said Mike.

"I hope you're not nasty to Greg," said his mother.

"I'm not," said Mike. "He's nasty to me."

"Greg has problems," said his mother.

"Greg gives everyone else problems," said Mike.

"Both his parents have been ill a lot," said his mother. "He's lived with three different aunts in the last four years. It's been difficult for him. He has low self-esteem."

"What does that mean?"

"It means he doesn't like himself much."

"I'm not surprised," said Mike.

"That's not very kind," said his mother.

"You don't know what he's like," said Mike. "He's a pain."

"He's just trying to get attention," said his father. "He doesn't know how to make friends."

It was somehow typical, Mike thought later, that the argument about Greg went on for so long that he wasn't able to leave early, after all, and Greg joined him at the usual place. It seemed Greg could be a nuisance even when he wasn't there.

The walk wasn't so bad, though, because Scott came to meet them. It was easier to ignore Greg when there was someone else there to talk to.

Not that Greg took the hint. He plodded along behind them, just too close, determined to hear everything they said.

Mike got the impression Scott was just a little disappointed to hear the rest of the night had been quiet.

"Whatever it is," Scott said, "it definitely doesn't like you, does it?"

"Well I don't like it, either," said Mike.

"Have you found out any more about the lodger?"

"No," said Mike. "How could I?"

"Have you got a lodger?" said Greg.

"No," said Mike.

"What we have to do," said Scott, "is work out what it wants. It definitely wants you out of your room, that's for sure."

"I could ask if I can have the spare room instead," said Mike. "But I don't know if that would help. What about all the other stuff?"

"What stuff?" said Greg. "What's happening?"

"It can't have been the dog that fixed the clock to chime," said Scott thoughtfully.

"You know what, though," said Mike,

"there can't have been a dog there. Those cats – they come through like they own the place."

"What are you on about?" said Greg.

"But it isn't exactly a real dog, is it?" said Scott. "It isn't a live dog."

"Even so, it would still spook the cats, wouldn't it?" said Mike. "It would scare them. It scares me!"

"I get it!" said Greg triumphantly. "Your house is haunted!"

Mike and Scott walked on in silence, each trying to make sense of the various things that had happened.

"I'm right, aren't I?" Greg persisted. "It's haunted, isn't it? Isn't it? Mike?"

"YES!" said Mike, exasperated.

"So what happens?" said Greg eagerly. "Does blood pour down the walls?"

"No."

"So what is it? You see a rotting corpse in an empty room? A severed hand runs across the carpet? The floor bulges up and something horrible bursts through?"

"No!"

"Well what, then?"

"Something creeps about at night and moves things," said Mike.

"*That* doesn't sound very frightening."

"Well it is," said Mike irritably. He turned to Scott. "Listen, don't tell anyone else," he said. "I don't want to talk about it until I've got it sorted. It makes me nervous."

"Right," said Scott.

"And don't you say anything, either," said Mike, glaring over his shoulder at Greg.

"Tell me about it properly," said Greg. "Tell me what's going on and I won't tell anyone else."

"No," said Mike. "Back off. It's nothing to do with you."

Because Greg was walking behind him, Mike didn't see his expression. If he had, he would probably have been surprised to see that Greg didn't look angry or belligerent. He looked, just for a very brief moment, as if he might cry.

When they got to school, Greg marched importantly ahead of them into the yard.

"Mike's a baby!" he announced loudly. "He thinks his house is full of monsters and werewolves!"

Chapter 6

Day Four, Later

Naturally, after Greg's announcement, everyone wanted to hear about the house. And the more Mike said he didn't want to talk about it, the more interested they became.

It was Scott who thought of a way out. "We were just winding Greg up," he said, super-casually.

This was doubly effective. First of all, the questions stopped. And secondly, Greg was so fed up, both with Scott and with Mike, that he didn't hang around for the walk home. He set off at speed as soon as the bell went. He was well out of sight by the time Mike reached the school gates.

"You going to be OK?" said Scott.

"Yes," said Mike. "I'll just keep sleeping in the spare room. That seems to do it."

"But we have to find out what's going on somehow," said Scott. "We have to do something about it."

"I don't see how we can," said Mike.

And he didn't. Then.

That evening, just as he and his parents had finished eating, the front doorbell rang.

Mike's father went through from the kitchen to answer it.

Mike tipped his chair back to listen. He wondered vaguely if Scott might have called round.

It wasn't Scott, though, it was a stranger. He heard her voice quite clearly.

"Hallo," she said. "My name's Nicola Dark. I'm sorry to bother you but I used to rent a room here. I just came to ask if there've been any letters for me?"

Mike leapt to his feet and hurried to the front door.

A girl was on the step, grown up but young. She was smiling and she looked friendly and normal.

"Yes," Mike's father was saying, "one came yesterday." He picked it off the hall table and handed it to her.

"Oh, thank you," said Nicola. "I have tried to tell everyone I've moved but there's always someone you forget, isn't there."

"Do you want to leave us a forwarding address?" said Mike's father. "In case we get any more."

"I've written it down already," said Nicola. She took a piece of paper out of her bag and handed it to him. "I'm only a couple of streets away," she said, "so I don't mind collecting it, but…"

"If anything else turns up, we'll re-address it," said Mike's father. "Save you calling round for nothing."

She was out of the gate and on the pavement by the time Mike had succeeded in convincing himself he had to talk to her.

"I – I just wanted to ask you something about the house," he said.

"Oh, yes?" Nicola didn't seem to mind.

She leaned on the wall and smiled at him.

"Well," said Mike, not sure where to begin. "You were a lodger here, right?"

"Yes, for almost a year."

"Which room was yours?"

"The big one at the front."

"Oh." said Mike. "That's my parents' room now."

Nicola nodded politely. She was beginning to look puzzled.

"Was there another lodger?" said Mike.

"Yes, my best friend Alison. We're sharing a flat now."

"Was she in the little room, at the front?"

"No, the big room at the back."

"The spare room," said Mike. "So who was in my room?"

"Mrs Mullish had the small room," said Nicola. "Mrs Mullish owned the house. She rented us the two bigger rooms so we could have chairs and a table each and not disturb her in her sitting-room." She gave Mike a very straight look. "There's something you're trying to find out," she said, "I can tell. Why don't you just ask me straight? I'll answer you if I can."

Mike took a deep breath. "Is this house haunted?" he said.

Nicola looked startled. "No," she said. "No, I'm sure it isn't. That is – I never noticed anything odd when I lived here. Nor did Alison, I'm sure. She'd have told me. It was a very nice place to live – apart from the chiming clock but we soon got used to that."

"Thank you," said Mike. He felt thoroughly confused. He somehow didn't think Nicola would lie to him. But how could she have lived here for nearly a year and not noticed anything strange?

"Why do you ask?" said Nicola. "What's happened? Did something frighten you?"

"No," said Mike. She was nice but he didn't want to tell her the stories. He was worried they might sound silly. "No – I – er – I just thought I heard someone say it was haunted."

"Who said that?"

"I – I can't remember."

"Well whoever it was, I'm sure they were mistaken."

"Right," said Mike.

"Is that it?" said Nicola. "You can ask anything you want, I don't mind."

"No," said Mike. "That's it. Thanks."

Although Nicola had seemed so normal, and so nice, Mike had had too many odd experiences to be truly reassured by what she had said. Even so, he went up to his room to do his homework. He wasn't ready to face an argument with his parents about whether or not he could shift himself into the spare room. He planned that, for a while, he would carry on sneaking in there to sleep after they'd gone to bed.

He was sitting at his desk staring at a history book when it happened.

The door, which he had left partly open, suddenly swung right open. In fact it swung so far open it was flat against the wall. Just before it hit the wall, it creaked.

It gave Mike a horrible fright. He got up from his desk and stood staring at the gaping door. For a moment, it remained where it was.

He decided a draught must have blown it. Then, as he watched, it swung the other way, until it was still wide open but now at right angles to the wall. Again, it creaked.

Mike had never heard his door creak before, but then he'd never opened it so wide before. It seemed it only creaked when it swung round on its hinges as far as it could go.

He was still wondering where the draught could be coming from when the door swung again, and again, right back against the wall, then at right angles to it. Right back. Right angles. Over and over again. And every time, the creak.

No draught could possibly behave like that. Something had to be moving the door – but there was nothing to be seen.

Mike was terrified. He didn't want to pass the swinging, creaking door to get out of the room, but he didn't want to stay in there alone, either. He tried to shout for his parents, but he was so scared his voice wouldn't work.

Swing, creak, swing, creak – the creaks were beginning to sound stranger and stranger. Suddenly he understood. The creaks weren't all the same, each one was slightly different.

The creaks were words!

He recognized "what" and then "do". He was almost too panicky to listen, but he managed to force himself.

That was when he heard the whole sentence – a sentence spoken entirely by the creaking of a swinging door:

"What – do – you – think – you – are – doing – in – here?" it said.

Chapter 7

Day Five

As soon as the creaking stopped, and he had the courage to pass through his own doorway, Mike's instinct was to run down into the kitchen to his parents.

He did run down, but when he got there he didn't tell them what had happened. It didn't seem likely they would take him seriously if he announced that his bedroom door had just asked him a question.

So he pretended he'd finished his homework and just hung around with them until it was time for bed.

Even though he crept through into the spare room again, and even though nothing else happened during the night, he was too nervous to sleep well.

Scott met him halfway to school, like the day before. Unlike the day before, though,

Greg didn't join them. He'd gone early, by himself.

"Right," said Scott, when he'd heard about Nicola and also about the sinister, creaking words. "We're getting warmer."

"We are? How?"

"It's obvious," said Scott. "*That's* why Mrs Mullish sold the house. She sold it because it's haunted and she couldn't take it any more. She was in your room, remember. That's where it all happens."

"Except for the clock – and stuff moving around in the kitchen…"

"Except for that," agreed Scott. "But it's *mostly* in your room, isn't it? That's why Nicola and what's-her-name didn't notice anything."

"You could be right," said Mike doubtfully.

"I am right."

"You said N. Dark was the cause of all the trouble," said Mike. "N. Dark and her Practices. But she wasn't. I'm absolutely certain she's not into anything like that."

"OK," said Scott. "So I was wrong about that. But I'm not wrong about this. You know what we have to do, don't you?"

"No."

"We have to go and see Mrs Mullish."

"What good's that going to do?"

"We get her to admit that's why she moved out," said Scott. "We get her to describe everything she saw and heard. And we persuade her to tell your mum and dad. They may not believe you, but they'd believe her."

"And then what?"

"Well..." said Scott, shrugging. "And then they do something about it."

"You said *we* had to do something about it."

"We will," said Scott. "As far as we can. Then we hand over to them for the last bit. It'll work ... trust me."

After school, Scott walked home with Mike. He wasted no time when they got there. He walked straight up to Mike's mother and said, in his most grown-up tones, "Do you have a forwarding address for Mrs Mullish, please?"

Mike's mother looked surprised. "No," she said. "We did everything through the estate agent."

"Which estate agent?" said Scott swiftly.

"Bilton and Groves," said Mike's mother.

Before she had time to ask why he wanted to know, Scott announced they were going for a walk, and hustled Mike out of the front door.

"The estate agent's never going to give her address to two kids," Mike objected, hanging back outside the High Street office.

"We can try," said Scott.

They went inside. They were faced with a large room with six desks in it. There was a person behind each desk. Five of them were talking on the telephone. One of them was gazing into space.

Amazingly, the woman who was gazing into space smiled and asked if she could help. She didn't seem at all put out that they were unlikely to be about to buy themselves a valuable piece of property.

She listened to Mike's enquiry and then pulled out the drawer of the filing cabinet beside her. "I think I remember that house," she said.

"Why?" said Scott eagerly. "Was there something weird about it?"

"No, but it was a recent sale." She took out a file and opened it. "Yes, here we are," she said. "The owner was a Mrs Mullish but her niece dealt with everything. I have an address in Canada for her." She looked up from the file and smiled at them both. "If you want to write to her, I'll be happy to send the letter on."

They thanked her and hurried outside.

"That's no good," said Mike. "Her niece is never going to write back to us, is she?"

"Probably not," said Scott. "Anyway, it'd all take too long." He looked sombre for a moment, then he brightened. "I know what," he said. "N. Dark! Nicola. She'll know where Mrs Mullish is. And you've got her address. She left her address with your dad, didn't she?"

Nicola's address was still on the hall table where Mike's father had left it, so there was no need to ask for it.

Mike raised his voice. "We're just going out," he said. "We won't be long."

"Out again!" said his mother, from the kitchen.

"Back in two seconds," Mike called, as they closed the door behind them.

Nicola was quite surprised to find them on her doorstep. Then she recognized Mike. "Hallo," she said. "I knew there was something else you wanted to ask me."

"There wasn't, then," said Mike. "But there is now. We need Mrs Mullish's address."

"I'm sorry," said Nicola, "I'm afraid I can't help you."

"We only want to talk to her for a few minutes," said Mike.

Nicola shook her head. "Mrs Mullish is dead," she said. "That's why Alison and I had to find somewhere else to live. She died and her niece came over from Canada and put the house up for sale."

Scott grabbed at Mike's arm. He was speechless.

Mike stood still for a few seconds with his mouth open. He looked as if his mind was totally empty but in fact a lot of thoughts were running through it.

Mrs Mullish had slept in his room. Mrs Mullish was dead. His room seemed to be haunted. You had to be dead to haunt. Round and round went the thoughts.

Then he remembered something that didn't quite fit. Those padding feet, the whining sound, the scratch marks on the door.

"Are you all right?" said Nicola. "Oh dear, did you know Mrs Mullish, was she a relative, have I given you an awful shock?"

"No," said Mike, recovering, more or less.

"No, we didn't know her. Can I ask you something else?"

"Of course."

"Did Mrs Mullish have a dog?"

"Yes," said Nicola. "Jed. A big mongrel, half alsation and half I-don't-know-what."

"But there are cat doors," said Mike.

"Lots of people in that road own cats," said Nicola, "but the houses are all joined together so there's no way through. Cats like to roam free, so Mrs Mullish let them walk through her house. She liked cats."

"But Jed...?"

"Jed was fine with cats," said Nicola. "He just ignored them."

Mike asked one last question. He asked it even though he was sure he knew the answer. "What happened to Jed?"

"Jed was totally devoted to Mrs Mullish," said Nicola. She looked quite sad. "He pined dreadfully when she died. He could never have settled with anyone else. The vet had to put him to sleep..."

Mike and Scott walked most of the way back to Mike's in silence.

It was Mike who spoke first. "I don't think that helped," he said.

"It did," said Scott firmly. "Now we know who's doing the haunting. It's Mrs Mullish and Jed."

"Yes, but we don't know how to stop them!" said Mike. "And that's what I want. I want them to go away! It's all right for you, you haven't been here when they're around. I tell you, they're REALLY frightening."

Chapter 8

Day and Evening Six

Mike secretly slept in the spare room for the third night.

He had really wanted Scott to stay over. In fact he had even told his parents why. "This house is haunted," he had said. "I won't be so scared if Scott's here too."

They told him not to be silly, and reminded him that sleepovers were never allowed during the school week.

"You'll talk half the night and be tired all day in class," said his mother. "Tomorrow's Friday – Scott can stay over tomorrow if his parents agree."

Mike wondered again if he should ask to change rooms officially, but decided not to. What if they said no?

So he spent a nervous two hours in his own room until he heard their door shut and could risk tiptoeing into the spare.

Just one more night, he thought, and then Scott would be here and perhaps, between them, they could sort things out. Somehow.

He lay awake for quite a long time, but nothing strange happened. Things were definitely better when he wasn't in his room.

It was true that there was a moment when he thought he heard something sniffing around the house wall, outside, below the spare room window. But when he peered out there was nothing to be seen and he convinced himself it was one of the cats. His parents had locked the cat doors again and they were probably trying to figure out some other way of getting through.

At school, there wasn't much chance to talk to Scott. They were both running late and arrived only seconds before the bell. At lunchtime there was football practice. After school they had to call in at Scott's to pick up his overnight bag. Then Scott's father drove them to Mike's home. Almost as soon as they arrived the food was on the table and they ate with Mike's parents.

Eventually, though, they escaped up to Mike's room, where the folding bed was all ready for Scott.

"I'm not sleeping in here tonight," Mike warned, as he sat down on the end of his own bed. "Not even with you. We'll both have to sneak across the landing later."

Scott sat at Mike's desk. "We have to stay here," he said. "This was her room. If we want to talk to her…"

"I don't want to talk to her!" said Mike. "I want her to go away."

"But we *have* to talk to her," said Scott, reasonably. "We have to find out what she wants. We have to try to fix it for her, *then* she'll go."

They sat in silence for a few moments.

Scott picked up one of Mike's felt-tips and began doodling on a piece of paper.

"She may not turn up this evening," said

Mike eventually. "She doesn't keep regular hours."

"Ghosts are like that," said Scott. He had doodled a row of football shirts.

"How do you know?"

"I've heard," said Scott. He chose more felt-tips and began colouring the football shirts in. "It's strange, isn't it?" he said. "Why do you suppose they only haunt at night?"

"*She* doesn't," said Mike. "She chucked my stuff out of this window in the middle of the afternoon."

"That's true. But mostly she's on the move in the night, isn't she?"

"I suppose it's because she's in another dimension," said Mike, after some thought. "Her timing isn't the same as ours. She doesn't live like we do."

"She doesn't live at all," said Scott, picking out a purple pen.

"I bet nothing happens this evening," said Mike.

Half of him wanted it to – so that Scott

would understand what he'd had to put up with. But half of him definitely didn't want it to. He hadn't enjoyed feeling frightened.

As he idly watched Scott colouring in a purple sleeve, he noticed that the rasping of the felt-tip on the paper sounded odd.

He didn't get it right away.

Then, suddenly, he did.

The scratching of the pen was somehow being manipulated. The ghost of Mrs Mullish was shaping the sounds into words.

"What – scratch – do – scratch – you ..."

Mike jumped to his feet. At the exact same moment, Scott realized what was going on. He leapt up and threw the pen as far from him as he could. It hit the door and fell to the ground, leaving a tiny purple dot on the woodwork. At once the door swung wide, and its creaking completed the sentence.

"What – do – you – think – you – are – doing – in – here?"

When the sentence was finished, the door stood still. It was almost closed.

Mike didn't quite know why he did it, but he climbed up on his bed. He stood there, trying not to shake. Scott joined him. But before they had time to decide whether to try and answer the question, they heard a completely new sound. It came again, and again, and again.

Something was padding steadily up the stairs towards Mike's bedroom door. They could hear its feet. They could hear its panting breath.

"I wish I was at home," Scott whispered.

"You're the one who said we had to talk to them," Mike hissed back.

As the footsteps reached the landing and approached the door, Scott stepped backwards, lost his balance and fell off the bed. As he hit the ground, the door flung itself wide and began to swing urgently to and fro again.

The footsteps stopped.

Then whatever was outside lifted its voice in a woeful cry which mingled with the horrible rhythmic creaking voice of the hinges.

Chapter 9

Evening Six, Later

....

Mike stood on the bed, clutching at the edge of the window-frame for support. Scott sat on the floor, where he'd fallen. They stared at the door as it swung to and fro. When it was at its widest open, they could both see out on to the landing. There was nothing there. Yet the crying sound continued. Something completely invisible was just outside the room, whining and scraping at the swinging door. The hinges were creak-speaking as they had before.

"Go downstairs, Jed," they said. *"You know you're not allowed up here."*

The scratching and whining stopped. Obediently, the unseen presence padded off down the stairs and into silence.

Mike prodded Scott's shoulder with his foot. "YOU said we had to talk to her – SAY something!"

"Hello," said Scott hoarsely, addressing the hinges.

"Explain yourselves!" grated the door.

Being talked to by an invisible dead person was bad enough, but the hinges made a particularly horrible sound. It set their teeth on edge. Mike jumped off the bed. "I can't stand it," he said. "We have to find her something better to speak with."

Later, he and Scott agreed they didn't know how they got themselves out of the room. They were not totally sure the dog had gone away, they couldn't see the shade of Mrs Mullish and they had a nasty feeling they might collide with something invisible but grisly in the doorway. To their surprise they got out with no trouble and made it to the kitchen.

"Great idea," said Scott. "Lots of things in the kitchen make a noise." He seized the blender. "This'll do," he said, heading for the stairs again. "Come on, Mike! We have to find out what she wants."

Later, they agreed they didn't know how they got themselves back into the room, either. But nothing blocked their way and Scott stood the blender on the desk, plugged it in, and switched on.

The steady hum of the blender was a definite improvement.

"Now, pay attention," it droned. *"I'm sure I've always made the house rules very clear, no one has misunderstood before. I do not rent out this room – never have and never will. It's mine. It's private."*

Mike opened his mouth to speak but the blender thrummed on. *"You may do as you please in the two rooms which I do rent out – you have free use of the bathroom – and you are permitted to cook for yourselves in the kitchen. But when in the kitchen, please do not throw away Jed's feeding bowl and do not bolt the cat-doors. The cats are allowed unrestricted access. Furthermore, it is not acceptable to rearrange my china. The mugs have always stood on the windowsill. Kindly do not put them in the cupboard. Finally, I do not permit tenants to switch off the clock chimes.*"

The blender hummed on wordlessly. Mrs Mullish was waiting for a response.

"But Mike lives here now," said Scott nervously.

"It's my room now," wailed Mike. He suddenly felt extremely sorry for himself and very hard done by. "My mum and dad said this was my room."

"*I think I may have been a little hasty,*" the blender whirred, "*throwing everything outside. I see you're only a child and you obviously believe you have a right to be in here. However, you are wrong about this. Kindly listen to this warning. If you do not extract all your belongings, AND yourself, I shall have you forcibly removed. And that is my last word.*"

And so it seemed to be. The blender spun on, but it simply made blending noises. It had no more to say.

Scott switched it off.

"She's gone," he said. His voice was a bit shaky.

Mike gave a huge relieved sigh. That sounded shaky, too.

Almost at once, there came the sound of feet treading steadily up the stairs again. Before either of them had time to panic, Mike's mother appeared in the doorway.

"Mike," she began, "have you seen my…"

She stopped abruptly as she caught sight of the blender.

"There it is!" she said. She marched across the room, unplugged it and hitched it under one arm. "What on earth were you doing with it?" she said, looking from one to the other of them.

There was a brief pause while Mike wondered whether to try her with the truth and see if she'd believe it.

She wasn't willing to wait, though.

"Honestly, Mike," she said. "Fancy taking my blender to play with! I'm beginning to lose patience with you!"

She turned and marched out of the room. The blender lead dangled out from under her arm like a tail.

There was a moment of startled silence. Then Scott said, "You know what the problem is, don't you?"

"Yes," said Mike. "I'm in deep trouble. I'm stuck in the middle of a haunting with my parents getting crosser and crosser with me by the minute."

"That's *a* problem," agreed Scott, "but it isn't *the* problem. *The* problem is that Mrs Mullish doesn't know she's dead."

Chapter 10

Day Seven

....

"What do you think she meant," said Mike anxiously, "when she said she'd have me 'forcibly removed'?"

"I don't know," said Scott. "But I don't think you'd like it."

"Well how long do you think I've got before she does it? Whatever it is?"

"Difficult to say," said Scott. "She's not on the same time-scale as us. I should think it could be ten seconds or a hundred years."

The two of them had shifted themselves into the spare room but they didn't go to sleep for a long time. They sat up until the early hours of Saturday morning. Most of the time they discussed the unique problems of Number 31. And all the time they listened out for disturbances. But there weren't any.

"She's waiting," said Mike miserably.

"She's waiting for me to leave home. I wonder when she'll guess I'm not going to."

"What *I* wonder," said Scott, looking thoughtful, "is why she can't speak."

"Because she's a ghost, of course!" said Mike.

"But Jed-the-dog is a ghost," said Scott. "And Jed can speak. He can whine, anyway."

"That's true," said Mike.

"I've been working it out," said Scott. "And I think I've got it!"

"You!" said Mike irritably. "YOU said N. Dark had definitely been doing magic in my room. Wrong! YOU said the problem was that thirty-one was thirteen backwards. Wrong again! YOU said if we talked to the ghost we could sort things out so she'd go away. Wrong three times!"

"I'm right about this, though," said Scott, unperturbed. "She can't talk because she doesn't know she's dead so she can't work her Ghostly Manifestation properly. But Jed *does* know he's dead, so he can."

"Maybe," said Mike, grudgingly.

"And I'll tell you something else," said Scott. "I think Jed knows *she's* dead. I think he's come back to fetch her. That's why he keeps whining at her door. He wants her to go with him."

"I wish she would," said Mike.

"Makes sense though, doesn't it?" said Scott.

"How can she possibly not know she's dead?" said Mike. "She must have noticed!"

"Well, she hasn't," said Scott, "and someone's got to tell her."

"How do you tell someone something like that!" said Mike. "That's really personal!"

They stared at each other in silence for a few seconds. Then Mike said hopefully, "Are you going to do it?"

"No," said Scott, without hesitation.

"Well, I'M not!" said Mike.

"SOMEONE has to," said Scott.

"Got any ideas?"

Scott looked thoughtful. Then he nodded

slowly. "Yes," he said. "Think about it! Who do we know who's good at telling people things they don't want to hear?"

A slow smile spread across Mike's face. "Greg!" he said.

"Greg," nodded Scott.

"So how do we get my parents out of the way while we do it?" said Mike. "Or do we let them watch?"

"We play it by ear," said Scott calmly.

It was hard to say who was more pleased when Mike and Scott announced at breakfast that they wanted Greg to come over – Mike's parents or, later, Greg himself.

In fact it was almost embarrassing.

Mike's parents even offered to take all three of them to the Leisure Centre in the afternoon. "We're going to the Antiques Fair in the big hall," said his mother. "But you three could go swimming. I think they have a flume."

Mike and Scott exchanged glances. "It's

OK, thanks," said Mike. "We'll just hang out in the garden."

"All right," said his mother. "But there are some very dark clouds blowing up. Be sure to come in BEFORE it rains – don't wait until your feet are all muddy."

Greg arrived just after Mike's parents had left.

"I didn't expect I'd ever see your house," he said to Mike in the hall. "I thought you didn't like me."

Mike felt a bit guilty. That in turn made him feel even more irritated by Greg than usual. "You're here, aren't you?" he said gruffly.

"My aunt says I annoy people," said Greg conversationally. "She says if I don't annoy you today maybe you'll ask me round again."

Scott and Mike looked at each other and shuffled uncomfortably.

"So what are we going to do, then?" said Greg.

There was a brief pause while Mike waited

for Scott to speak and Scott waited for Mike. Then, both speaking at once and interrupting each other, they told him.

"OK," said Greg, when they'd finished.

Neither of them had expected him to agree so readily.

"You're sure you understand?" said Mike.

Greg shrugged. "No problem," he said. "It doesn't sound like much of a haunting. No blood, no luminous slime, no severed hands, nobody with their heads swivelling round and round…"

"And you'll definitely do it?" said Scott. "You'll definitely tell her?"

"Sure," said Greg.

"We'd better get on with it, then," said Mike. "Where shall we do it?"

"She spends most of her time in your room," said Scott.

"No, thank you!" said Mike. "If something goes wrong and I'm in there she'll probably vaporize me. We'll do it in the sitting-room." He marched in decisively. "We know she comes in here to switch on the clock."

"If I get rid of her fast," said Greg, following him, "can I still stay over and hang out with you?"

"Yes," said Mike reluctantly.

"Right!" said Greg.

He walked into the centre of the sitting-room, drew a deep breath, windmilled his arms as if he was directing a plane in to land, and began to shout. "Hey, old woman!" he bellowed. "You're dead, OK? You've had it! You're history! Shove off!"

He dropped his arms to his sides and grinned at Mike and Scott. "There!" he said. "So now what shall we do?"

They stared at him blankly.

Then Mike said to Scott, "What if she doesn't turn up?"

"We have to make sure she does," said Scott.

"How do we do that?"

Greg looked from one to the other of them. "What are you on about?" he said.

"I've been thinking," said Scott to Mike. "She's never done anything in here except change the clock, has she?"

"I don't think so."

Scott nodded. "That's because your parents bought her stuff and it still looks like it did when she was alive," he said. "So what we have to do is mess it up. She'll turn up to sort it out and we can set Greg on her, right?"

"Right!" said Mike. He seized the end of the sofa and began to push it. Scott grabbed the other end and they turned it completely back to front.

Greg watched. "I thought this was just a game," he said.

They ignored him.

Scott turned the armchairs round the wrong way.

Mike put the padded footstool in the empty fireplace.

All Greg's bounce had gone out of him. He reversed across the room until his back was against the wall.

"You mean you're *really* calling something up?" he said.

Outside the clouds were gathering. There was a distant roll of thunder.

"Well, it won't work if she isn't here, will it?" said Scott impatiently. He threw all the cushions on the floor.

"Do you think the dog'll come too?" said Mike. He opened the doors of the glass-fronted cupboard and turned a small table upside down.

"It's getting very dark in here," said Greg in a small voice. "Can we put the lights on?"

"Yes," said Mike. He'd been so busy wrecking the room he'd forgotten to be nervous. Now, he remembered.

Before he could move, though, he was hit by an enormous wave of anger that flooded across the room. It was just like the anger he'd felt in the kitchen, but stronger, much, much stronger.

"Phooo!" said Scott, who'd felt it too.

"I want out!" said Greg, pushing himself off from the wall and heading for the door.

"No, wait, you promised…" said Mike, grabbing his arm.

At that moment the padded footstool lifted itself out of the fireplace and flew through the air. As it landed with a thud, in its usual place on the carpet, a long drawn-out howl echoed around the hall and in at the sitting-room door.

Chapter 11

Day Seven, Later

The thunder rumbled closer.

"I can't do this!" breathed Scott. "I can't be afraid of thunder and a ghost at the same time. My head'll explode."

One after the other the cushions flew through the air and landed on the sofa and chairs.

The invisible dog had stopped howling but its bark sounded out, first from one corner of the room and then from another, as though it was circling them.

"Quick!" gasped Mike, who had backed so far into the fireplace he looked as if he was trying to get up the chimney. "Do something before she finishes clearing up and has me forcibly removed!"

Outside, lightning flickered and rain started to pour down.

Greg opened his mouth but no sound came out.

"Can you hear us?" croaked Scott, talking in the direction of the sofa which was revolving jerkily back into its proper position.

"She needs sound to talk with," said Mike. On an impulse he staggered to the television and switched it on.

Instantly, Scott flung himself at the set and turned it off again. "You can't have it on in a storm," he said. "If the aerial's hit, it'll catch fire!"

The upside-down table reversed itself right beside Greg, who was so jellified with terror that he looked as though he would never recover.

"Are you listening to us?" Mike called desperately. "We have to tell you something..."

The hissing of the rain caught his attention. It sounded peculiar, different.

"She's using the rain-sound," he choked. "Listen! What's she saying?"

"It's not loud enough," said Scott, dodging out of the way as the doors of the glass-fronted cupboard slammed shut.

"It'll be loud enough outside," said Mike, heading for the door. "Quick! Into the garden."

They ran, all three of them, the barking following at their heels.

"It's coming with us!" moaned Greg. "I thought we were escaping."

Outside the rain was falling steadily and the dark sky was glimmering with sheet lightning.

"We can't go out," Scott gabbled. "What if the lightning strikes?"

They stood, jammed together in the open back doorway, and shuddered as something swished through the kitchen wall into the garden, without bothering to use the door or the window. For the first time they could see shadowy disturbances in the air – shimmering against the curtain of rain – the vague and blurry outlines of a tall woman and a large mongrel dog.

The shadowy woman moved towards Mike. *"Trespasser,"* hissed the rain. *"Vandal! Trying to destroy my home. Go on, Jed, go for him, boy!"*

As the shadow-dog moved towards Mike, Greg found his voice.

"You're not really there," he squeaked.

"Shush!" swished the rain. *"THIS boy is the source of all the trouble."*

The shade of Jed reached Mike's side.

"Oh, help, do something!" said Scott.

"Listen to me!" Greg gasped desperately.

Mike stood rigidly as Jed sniffed his hand.

"You're fortunate Jed is a gentle dog," whispered the shade of Mrs Mullish.

"YOU'RE STUPID!" bellowed Greg.

That did it.

The shadow-woman turned from Mike and bore down on Greg.

"How dare you!" she rained.

"There's something important you have to know," said Greg, his voice quavering. "If you won't listen it isn't fair!"

"*I have ALWAYS been fair,*" swished Mrs Mullish. "*I'm listening.*"

"You're dead," said Greg simply. "That's why you can turn the rain into words – that's why you can walk through walls – that's why other people have moved into your house..." Sudden inspiration struck him. "That's why you don't need to eat any more," he finished.

The vague outline of Mrs Mullish hovered silently in front of him.

Lightning flickered closer and a roll of thunder followed almost at once.

Everything and everyone, including the two who weren't quite there, seemed to wait for a long, tense moment.

Then phantom-Jed padded over to phantom-Mrs Mullish, looked up at her and whined. He sat as if he was begging and whined again. Then he dropped on to all fours, took the hem of her phantom-skirt in his phantom-jaws and gave a gentle tug.

"Your dog's dead, too," said Greg. He suddenly didn't feel afraid any more. His voice sounded quite kind. "It's all right," he said, "your dog knows where you should go – he's trying to lead you."

Mike gulped.

Scott sniffed.

Greg waited.

"Oh, my goodness, I think you're probably right," said Mrs Mullish in a perfectly normal voice.

The crash of thunder right overhead was so incredibly loud that they all jumped. At exactly the same moment a jagged line of lightning linked the garden with the clouds above for one single second. And in that second they all three saw the same thing – Mrs Mullish striding purposefully up the line of light with Jed bounding ahead of her, tail wagging enthusiastically.

The edge of the storm passed overhead and the sky began to lighten. The rain still fell but the drops were smaller and further apart.

"He did it!" said Scott. "Greg did it!"

"Thanks, Greg," said Mike.

The three of them stood together, staring up at the sky.

"Where do you think they've gone?" said Mike.

"To the next dimension," said Scott.

Greg turned away. "That's all you wanted me for," he said sulkily. "I'm going now."

"You can hang out with us, if you want," said Mike gruffly. "Just don't push, OK?"

"And don't make annoying remarks," said Scott.

The rain faded away. The sky grew lighter. There was a faint sound of faraway thunder. But there were no words in it.

A huge sense of relief flooded over them all.

Then, "Your garden's really small, isn't it?" said Greg. "You couldn't play football out here or anything."

Scott frowned.

Mike glowered.

"Small but nice," said Greg hastily. "Very

nice. We could practice fancy-footwork and dribbling…"

Scott relaxed.

Mike nodded. "I'll get the ball," he said. As he went into the house he noticed that it seemed lighter, happier. And as he pulled the football out from under his bed he realized that his room really was HIS room. At last.

THE GREAT PIG SPRINT
Judy Allen

At first, Kate's not sure about Lee Road City Farm. But then she makes friends with a goat called Cleopatra and soon she finds herself involved in planning a Summer Open Day, with a highly original scheme for raising money!

"Good, earthy reading for juniors interested in ponies, pigs and poultry." *Books for Keeps*

SPOOKS AHOY!
Mary Hooper

A narrowboat weekend on the river is the setting for this hilarious follow-up to *Spook Spotting*, featuring Amy, the girl with the over-active imagination and her birdwatching best friend, Hannah. From the moment Mum mentions the boating holiday, Amy's mind goes overboard with thoughts of treasure, mermaids, phantom ships and adventure on the high seas. The reality, however, turns out to be quite different – but still with thrills, spills and laughs aplenty!

CREEPE HALL
Alan Durant

"Vampires, ghosts and werebadgers... A fast-moving story – loads of fun, written with style and humour." *Books for Keeps*

"An amusing, gently prodding tale in the Addams Family tradition."
The Independent on Sunday

"This book is really excellent." *Kids Out!*

THE CURSE OF THE SKULL
June Crebbin

Jack's best friend Tom is mad about bones. He's got a huge collection of animal skulls and skeletons – mice, cows, sheep... But when Tom takes a human skull from some earthworks in the local church, Jack thinks he's gone too far. He's sure the skull will bring down a curse on them. And then things do indeed start to go wrong... This humorous spooky tale will tingle your spine and tickle your funny bone!

SMART GIRLS
Robert Leeson

They're witty, they're wise – you can't pull the wool over these girls' eyes!

"Five folk tales from across the world simply and skilfully retold... The stories are lively and funny." *Gillian Cross, The Daily Telegraph*

"Entertaining, thought-provoking and a source of invaluable learning." *Books for Keeps*

Shortlisted for the Guardian Children's Fiction Award.

MORE WALKER PAPERBACKS
For You to Enjoy